LEVEL 1 READER

W9-ARC-168

Little Big HORSE

WHERE'S MY BIKE?

MCL FOR
NEPTUNE CITY
PUBLIC LIBRARY

Written and Illustrated by Dave Horowitz

SCHOLASTIC INC.

I can't wait
for class
to be over.

Finally.

To the bikes!

Where is my bike?
I left it right here.

There goes Pablo.

Hey—wait a minute.

That's my bike.

"Finders keepers,"
he says.

I can't believe
he just took
my bike.

It's not fair.

But, wait . . .
What's this?

It's Pablo.
And he's all
alone, crying.

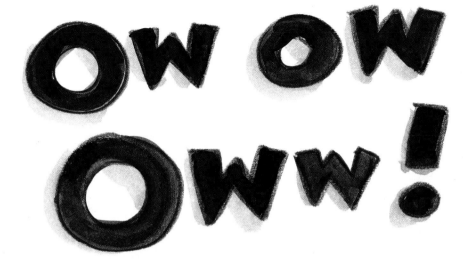

"I fell off my bike,"
he says.

"No! You fell off *my* bike," I say. "Why'd you take my bike?"

"Because my bike is broken," he says. "And now yours is, too."

It's not even broken.

It's only a flat.

We take my bike
to Smitty's and
fix it right up.

Then we go fix
Pablo's bike.

"Sorry about
before," he says.

"Forget about it,"
I say. And off

we go . . .

Learn more about the author at
horowitzdave.com.

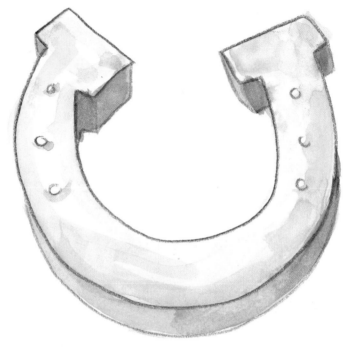

No part of this publication may be reproduced, stored in a retrieval system,
or transmitted in any form or by any means, electronic, mechanical,
photocopying, recording, or otherwise, without written permission
of the publisher. For information regarding permission,
write to Scholastic Inc., Attention: Permissions Department,
557 Broadway, New York, NY 10012.

ISBN 978-0-545-49214-0

Copyright © 2014 by Dave Horowitz.
All rights reserved. Published by Scholastic Inc.

SCHOLASTIC and associated logos are trademarks and/or
registered trademarks of Scholastic Inc.

12 11 10 9 8 7 6 5 4 3 2 1   14 15 16 17 18 19/0

Printed in the U.S.A.   40
First printing, January 2014

Designed by Paul W. Banks